Octopus
All octopuses have eight long arms.

Panther grouper
These fish will eat other small fish.

Seahorse
The seahorse uses its tail to secure itself to rocks and plants.

Tropical fish
There are hundreds of different kinds of fish around coral reefs.

Unlike almost all other fish, seahorses swim upright.

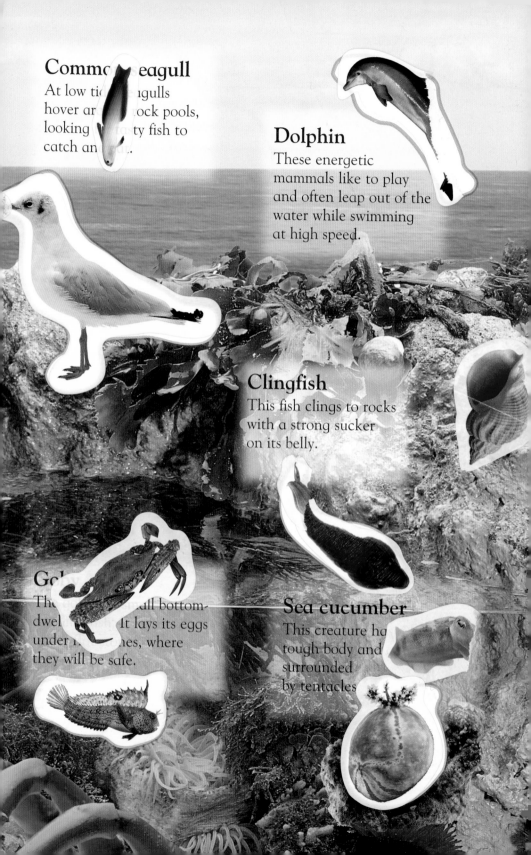

Common seagull
At low tide, seagulls
hover around rock pools,
looking for tasty fish to
catch and eat.

Dolphin
These energetic
mammals like to play
and often leap out of the
water while swimming
at high speed.

Clingfish
This fish clings to rocks
with a strong sucker
on its belly.

Goby
The goby is a small bottom-
dweller. It lays its eggs
under rock ledges, where
they will be safe.

Sea cucumber
This creature has a
tough body and is
surrounded
by tentacles.

Dolphin

The dolphin's streamlined body helps it to swim fast through the ocean currents.

Sea anemones can be found in rock pools.

Limpet

A strong, suckerlike foot enables the limpet to attach itself very firmly to rocks around the shore.

Fiddler crab

This kind of crab likes to burrow in the sand. It emerges to feed at low tide.

Harlequin sweetlips
This fish swims with
its tail up.

Angelfish
Many types of angelfish
live on the reef.

Bulging eyes
This fish has bulbous
yellow-rimmed
eyes.

Many fins
This red-and-white
striped tropical fish
has seven fins.

Colorful coral reefs grow in warm, tropical seas.

Great white

The great white
shark is the biggest
meat-eating fish.

The octopus's long, curly tentacles have suckers.

Sea and shore

All kinds of interesting creatures live in and around the ocean. Warm rock pools on the seashore make ideal homes for crabs, starfish, and other seaside creatures. The oceans are full of fish and home to mammals such as the dolphin.

Sandcastle

The best place to build a sandcastle is near the water's edge. Here, the sand is moist and easy to mold.

Waving tentacles

Sea anemones look like plants, but are actually animals. They use stinging tentacles to catch prey.

Blennies live around rocks in shallow water.

The blacktip reef shark hunts on the outer edges of the reef.

Butterfly fish
Butterfly fish can have many different patterns.

Forceps fish
This bright fish has a very long snout.

Starfish
The five-armed starfish lives on the coral reef.

Silver fish

This shiny fish has
a pointed snout. Its
scales look like they
are made of silver.

Squid

A squid has ten arms for
grasping food and a thick
shell inside its soft body.
The squid can swim
very fast.

Seaweed is a source of food for many sea creatures.

Sea slugs

Sea slugs are like snails
but they do not have shells.
Some are brightly colored.

A whale's tail br___ ___ace as it dives for food.

Whale
Like dolphins, whales also surface in order to breathe air.

Dogfish
This small kind of shark is called a dog fish because it hunts and travels in a pack, like dogs do.

Twinspot wrasse
This fish gets its name from the two large spots on its body. If it senses danger, it will burrow down into the sea bed to hide.

Starfish
Most starfish have five arms. They eat oysters and other shellfish along the shore.

Triggerfish
Divers should avoid
this poisonous fish.

The spots help to camouflage the ray on the sea bed.

Sea snake
These glide through the water.

Clownfish
These colorful fish live
in the tentacles of
sea anemones.

Giant clam
Clams can close their
shells.

Dolphins communicate using squeaks and clicking sounds.

Hourglass dolphin
This beautiful dolphin travels in groups of six or more, and feeds on small fish.

Common lobster
This kind of lobster sometimes gets washed up in rock pools. They use their long antennae to feel their way around.

Coral reef

Some of the brightest and most beautiful creatures on Earth live in our oceans—especially around the coral reefs. Some creatures look so bizarre and colorful, its hard to believe they are real!

Box jellyfish
The jellyfish has stinging tentacles.

Scuba diver
Special breathing equipment, such as oxygen tanks, let divers stay underwater for a long time.

Puffer fish
These fish blow up like a balloon when they sense danger.

Stonefish
Hidden in the rocks, this is the most venomous fish of all.